RED

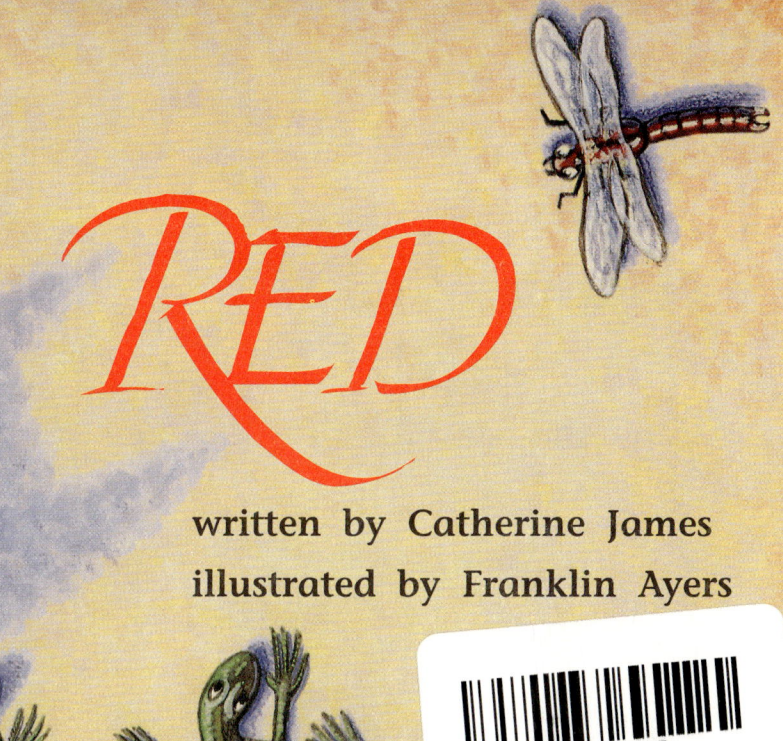

written by Catherine James
illustrated by Franklin Ayers

HARCOURT BRACE & COMPANY
Orlando   Atlanta   Austin   Boston   San Francisco   Chicago   Dallas   New York
Toronto   London

In the morning Red left her house. "See you later, Red," said Mrs. Bensen.

"My goodness, Red looks fat," Mrs. Bensen said to herself.

Red saw her friends and found some treats. "See you later, Red," they said.

"My goodness, Red looks fat," they said to each other.

5

That night
Red did not
come home.
Mrs. Bensen got
out of bed and
looked for Red.

7

"My goodness, Red," Mrs. Bensen said.